DIVINE WONDER

Laura Shenton

DIVINE WONDER

Laura Shenton

Iridescent Toad Publishing

Iridescent Toad Publishing.

Cover by Cyan Book Cover Design.

First edition. ISBN: 978-1-913779-92-4

Chapter One

"Shit!" Jess yelped as the searing heat of the plate seeped through her skin.

She hadn't expected it to be so hot. The sudden sensation had caught her off guard.

"Careful, Jess!" the chef barked from behind a sizzling pan, sweat beading on his furrowed brow. "That plate's hotter than the Devil's arsehole."

Jess clenched her jaw, suppressing a snarl at the chef's crude remark. She didn't need any reminders about the damn heat of the plate. Her fingers throbbed like they'd been slammed in a car door. As the pain radiated through her hand, she could almost hear the mocking laughter of the kitchen staff echoing around her.

She forced herself to maintain a firm grip on the

plate despite the pain. Some of the serving staff glanced at her with a mixture of curiosity and concern – she was certain that they were talking about her behind her back.

"Jesus Christ, Jess, you're gonna burn your fingers off," one of the line cooks chided, rolling his eyes at her as he flipped a perfectly seared steak onto a plate. "Just use a damn towel."

"Thanks for the advice," she snapped.

Jess grabbed a white linen towel to wrap around the scalding plate. She could still feel the heat pulsating through the fabric like a volcano.

"Are you ok, hun?" Adele asked sweetly, feigning concern as she sauntered over, her eyes wide with faux-innocence.

Jess hated Adele's fake smile and the way she always acted like she was so much better than everyone else.

"Nothing's wrong, Adele," Jess snapped, forcing herself to stay focused on the plate rather than her annoying co-worker. "I've got it under control."

"Sure you do, hun," Adele replied, her voice dripping with condescension. "Just remember, the customer is waiting for their food. You don't want to make them wait too long."

"Thanks for the fucking newsflash," Jess retorted.

She tried to ignore the smug expression plastered across Adele's face, but the fact that she had to deal with this bullshit on top of her already shitty day was infuriating.

As she watched Adele leave the kitchen to serve her own table, Jess' mind raced with thoughts of what she could do to get back at her tormentor. A flick of her wrist could set Adele's hair alight or ignite the napkins on the tables. But she knew deep down that she couldn't give in to those dark desires. She had to maintain control over her abilities, lest she reveal herself as the very monster society despised – a paranormal, a freak, a menace to be feared and shunned.

"Alright, let's go, Jess! Chop-chop!" the chef shouted impatiently, gesturing towards the dining area with his spatula.

"Fine," Jess muttered.

Gripping the towel-wrapped plate with as much force as she could muster, she took a deep breath and prepared to face the discerning gaze of the restaurant's wealthy patrons, her powers simmering just beneath the surface like a pot about to boil over.

With a smouldering glare, Jess swallowed her anger and focused on the task at hand. Losing this job would only make life harder, and she couldn't afford to let her temper or powers get the better of her. Not now. Not with the rent due and with groceries dwindling.

She tried to centre herself as she looked down at the steaming plate before her. The aroma of seared steak and sautéed vegetables wafted up to her nose, momentarily distracting her from her hatred of the task at hand. If she could just make it through this shift, she could then retreat to her cramped apartment and forget all about the stifling atmosphere of the high-end restaurant and its snobby clientele.

"Come on, Jess," she muttered under her breath. "You've dealt with worse."

She pushed through the kitchen doors, and as she navigated through the dining area, her senses were assaulted by the overwhelming wealth on display. The chandelier above cast a warm glow upon the rich mahogany tables and opulent silk tablecloths. Serving staff in crisp white shirts moved gracefully between patrons.

Jess passed a middle-aged man with greying hair. His tailored suit was probably worth more than her entire wardrobe.

"Excuse me," she murmured.

He glanced down at her with a sneer, his lips curled in contempt.

"Watch where you're going, girl," he snapped, his voice dripping with disdain. "You're here to serve us, not to get in our way."

"Sorry, Sir," she replied, her voice barely hiding her frustration.

Inwardly she raged. She was fed up with the continuous judgement from people who knew nothing about her life or her struggles.

"Can't even find decent help these days," she overheard another patron mutter.

Jess tightened her grip on the plate, her knuckles turning white. The heat radiating from it seeped into her arm, but she pushed through the pain as she focused on getting to her table.

"Finally," a well-dressed woman said with a sigh, the irritation evident in her voice. "I was beginning to think you'd forgotten about us."

"I apologise for the wait, Madam," Jess said as she forced a smile.

She placed the plate before the customer, trying to ignore the throbbing sensation in her hand.

The woman huffed and then turned her attention back to her dining companions.

As Jess made her way back to the kitchen, her anger continued to simmer. She couldn't help but feel a heavy weight settling on her chest as she wove her way through the sea of critical gazes. This job was essential for her survival, and yet every shift felt like a battle to maintain her composure, to keep her powers in check. She gritted her teeth, fighting back the urge to lash out. Losing control would not only out her as a paranormal; it would confirm everyone's worst fears about people like her.

Ignoring the kitchen staff, she grabbed another unpleasantly hot plate and quickly made her way to the next table.

"Here you are," she said, her voice strained as she approached.

"Excuse me!" the elderly woman's voice cut through the commotion, her shrill tone dripping with disapproval. "I ordered the salmon, not this!"

Jess clenched her jaw, trying to swallow the bitter resentment that bubbled in her throat like molten lava. With a tight-lipped smile, she forced herself to meet the woman's icy gaze.

"I apologise for the mix-up, Madam," she said, her voice failing to conceal the storm brewing within. "I'll fix it right away."

"See that you do," the woman demanded, lifting her chin imperiously.

Jess' heart pounded in her ears, drowning out the murmur of the other diners as she strode back towards the kitchen, each step an exercise in self-control. She could feel the eyes of the restaurant's well-heeled patrons boring into her back.

Fuck 'em, she thought viciously. *Like they've never made a goddamn mistake before.*

As she reached the kitchen doors, Jess paused for a moment to steady herself. She couldn't afford to lose it now – not when she was so close to the end of her shift, so close to escaping the suffocating confines of this place for another day.

Ok, she told herself. *You've got this. Just get the damn salmon and get out.*

With renewed determination, Jess pushed through the swinging doors, her eyes scanning the chaotic kitchen for the elusive dish. After a few tense moments, she spotted a perfectly prepared plate of salmon resting on the pass, just waiting to be served.

"Finally," she said with a sigh as she used a towel to grab the plate. "Maybe now I can get through this shift without any more shit."

With a grim smile, Jess re-entered the dining area, carefully weaving between tables as she made her way back towards the irate elderly woman.

"Here you go," she said through gritted teeth, trying her best to keep her voice steady as she bent down to place the plate on the table.

In her urgent need to get the job over and done with, Jess felt the plate slip from her fingers. She watched in horror as the steaming food slid off. The hollandaise sauce oozed across the pristine white tablecloth before landing, along with the salmon, on the woman's lap.

"You absolute moron!" the elderly woman screeched. "What on earth do you think you're doing?! You've ruined my dress!"

Staring at the mess she'd made, and at the seething woman before her, Jess felt the last of her self-control snap like a twig. Her thoughts flitted between the desire to apologise profusely and the overwhelming urge to unleash the full force of her fury upon the entire restaurant.

"Shit, shit, shit," she whispered.

A torrent of murmurs and gasps echoed around the room in a cacophony of judgment. Her every breath catching in her throat as she grappled with a combination of rage and dread, Jess' vision tunnelled.

"Look what you've done!" the woman shouted, gesturing wildly at her ruined dress. "You useless girl!"

"I'm so sorry," Jess rambled.

"Sorry isn't good enough!" the woman retorted, her eyes alight with indignation. "I demand to speak to your manager!"

"Of course," said Jess, knowing that she had no choice but to comply.

The familiar heat of humiliation burned in her cheeks. She knew what the consequences of this disaster would be: another complaint, another mark against her name, inching her ever closer to losing the job she so desperately needed.

"Jess, what the hell is going on here?" the voice of the restaurant owner, Mr Rossiter, boomed out across the dining area as he stormed over towards the incident.

"Sir, there was an accident," Jess tried to explain.

"Accident?! More like outright incompetence," the woman interjected, her eyes narrowing as she glared at Jess. "I want her fired!"

"Please, Sir," Jess begged, frantically gripping the edge of the table as if it could anchor her to sanity. "It was a mistake. I'll do whatever it takes to make it right."

'Whatever it takes' echoed in her mind, a reminder of the lengths she was willing to go to in order to survive; it was the price she'd pay to keep her job in a city that always had more candidates than vacancies.

"Jess, I don't know what's got into you lately," said Mr Rossiter, his voice heavy with disappointment. "But this can't keep happening. Clean up this mess and then meet me in my office."

"Y-yes, Sir," Jess stuttered, the weight of her mistake settling upon her shoulders like an iron shroud.

Get yourself together, she told herself as she retreated towards the kitchen. *You have to.*

18

Chapter Two

"I can't believe this," Jess muttered to herself as she slung her bag over her shoulder.

As she shoved her way through the doors of the restaurant, the cool night air hit her face with a welcome sting. It did nothing to alleviate her annoyance though.

She had never been sent home early before, and it frustrated her to no end. What was the point in working so hard if they were just going to cut her hours like that?

"Hey, Jess!" a voice called out from further down the street.

Startled, Jess whirled around and found herself face-to-face with Tom, her cousin and closest confidant.

"Jesus Christ, Tom! You scared the shit out of me. What are you doing here?" she snapped, her nerves still frayed from work.

"Whoa, chill out! I just happened to be passing by. I thought you still had a few hours left of your shift. Are you ok?" he asked, his tone fuelled with concern.

"Just some bullshit with my boss," Jess replied, attempting to brush off the question.

"One of those days, huh?" said Tom. "Never mind. It won't matter in a hundred years' time. It probably won't even matter this time next year."

Jess couldn't help but smile at Tom's words. Their bond was strong. They shared everything with each other – laughter, tears, secrets... Well, almost everything. There was just one truth that she had always kept from him: the paranormal power she possessed.

She couldn't help but feel a twinge of guilt. Her abilities had been an integral part of her life for as long as she could remember, yet the thought of opening up about them felt as daunting as the thought of standing naked in front of a crowd –

perhaps more so!

Jess sensed that one day, she would have to tell Tom. But for now, she kept her secret hidden, just like the electricity that hummed beneath her skin, waiting to be unleashed.

"Thanks, Tom," she said softly, her frustration momentarily subsiding. "You always know what to say."

"Hey, it's what I do," he replied with a grin. "Now, let's go and grab some coffee and have a catch-up, yeah?"

As they walked, Jess couldn't help but think about her hidden powers and how they made her different from everyone else. Having to work so hard to keep them under control always made a difficult shift at work even tougher. How would people react if they knew she was one of those paranormals – outcasts with extraordinary abilities? Would they shun her? Hate her?

"Jess, are you alright?" Tom asked as they entered the coffee shop. "You've been quiet."

"Uh, yeah, just... thinking about work," she lied.

The scent of freshly brewed coffee filled the air, mingling with the sound of quiet chatter from patrons seated in the cosy booths.

"Don't be too hard on yourself about work," Tom said. "You're doing the best you can, and I've got your back, remember?"

"Thanks, Tom," Jess replied with a small smile, appreciating his support.

"Besides, you must be doing something right if they're letting you go home early," Tom continued as he gestured towards the counter. "Think of it as an unexpected break."

"Break, my arse," Jess muttered under her breath as they approached the counter.

Although Tom's optimism wasn't entirely lost on her, she couldn't afford to lose her job. Not when the rent was due, and she had bills to pay.

"Two coffees, please," Tom said to the barista before turning his attention back to Jess. "So, what's been going on at work, huh? You've been really stressed lately."

"Same old shit," Jess said with a sigh as she

accepted the cup of hot coffee from the barista. "Just... customers, y'know? They can be such arseholes sometimes."

"Tell me about it," Tom agreed, taking a sip of his own drink. "But hey, at least you're not dealing with them now, right?"

"True," Jess conceded, allowing herself a small chuckle.

It felt good to vent her frustrations and share a laugh with Tom. He always knew how to put things into perspective and make her feel better.

"Look, I know it's been tough lately," he said, his voice sincere as they sat down at a booth near the window. "But you're strong, Jess. You can handle anything that life throws at you."

The dim light from an overhead bulb cast shadows across Jess' face, highlighting the dark circles under her eyes. She ran her fingers through her tangled hair and took a long sip of coffee, relishing in its bitterness.

As they continued to chat, she couldn't shake the feeling that she was living on borrowed time. The weight of her secret hung heavily around her neck, threatening to suffocate her with its burden. She had come so close to losing it several times in that work shift from hell.

"Hey, Jess," said Tom, glancing at the clock on the wall. "Your bus is in ten minutes, remember?"

"Shit, you're right," she said. "Thanks for reminding me."

She took a final gulp of coffee and quickly started to gather her things. She'd been so lost in thought that she had practically forgotten about the time.

"No problem," said Tom, his warm eyes reflecting concern. "Just trying to make sure you get home safe. You know how I worry."

"Sometimes too much," Jess teased, attempting to lighten the mood.

Deep down, she appreciated Tom's care, even if it did feel a little suffocating at times. It was rare to find someone who genuinely cared in this harsh and unforgiving city.

"Better too much than not enough, right?" he

replied with a shrug, giving her a half-smile.

"True," Jess agreed as she zipped up her jacket and adjusted the strap of her bag on her shoulder. "Catch you later, then."

She looked around the small coffee shop one last time before heading towards the door.

"Take care, Jess," Tom called after her.

Jess stepped out into the chilly night air, a shiver running down her spine as she pulled her jacket tighter around her. The dull orange glow of the streetlamps cast eerie shadows onto the cracked pavements. She could hear the distant hum of traffic and the occasional outburst of drunken laughter from the bar down the street, but otherwise, the night was still and quiet.

The streets were littered with crumpled newspapers and discarded takeaway containers – remnants of the city's daily chaos. But there was something else that caught Jess' eye: a series of anti-paranormal posters plastered on the wall of a nearby building.

'*Stay vigilant,*' one warned. It featured a sinister caricature of a paranormal, their eyes glowing maniacally. *'Keep our city safe from the paranormal menace!'* commanded another, its illustration a snarling figure with lightning bolts for hands.

"Great," Jess muttered sarcastically, rolling her eyes. "Just what I need to see right now."

She knew all too well that the hatred towards paranormals was deeply ingrained in the city's psyche. People feared what they didn't understand, and that included supernatural powers. She couldn't help but feel a twinge of bitterness at the blatant discrimination. But there was no time to dwell on it; after the day she'd had, she just wanted to go home.

Get your head in the game, Jess, she admonished herself.

As she approached the bus stop, she felt a prickle of unease crawl up her spine. The hairs on the back of her neck stood on end. She couldn't shake the feeling that she was being watched. She forced herself to keep walking, her hurried footsteps echoing against the pavement.

She couldn't help but look around. Immediately she noticed a burly man leaning against a nearby wall. He was watching her intently with a sneer. She shuddered, but she kept walking, forcing herself to maintain a steady pace and not to look back.

"Hey, sweetheart," the man called out, his voice dripping with sleaze. "Where are you off to in such a hurry?"

"None of your damn business," Jess snapped back, trying to sound confident despite her mounting unease.

"Feisty, aren't we?" he said with a chuckle as he stepped forward to block her path. "How about you come with me? I'll show you a good time."

"Back off," Jess warned, her voice wavering slightly.

She could feel the electricity pumping around her body, pulsing just beneath the surface, begging to be unleashed. But she couldn't risk it, not here.

"Aww, don't be like that," the man said, reaching out to grab her arm. "I just want to..."

"Leave me alone!"

The words tumbled from Jess' lips with more force than she had intended. The man hesitated for a moment, clearly caught off guard by her sudden defiance.

"Or what?" he chided, regaining his composure. "You'll call the police? You think they'll care?"

Jess clenched her fists, her anger at boiling point. She took a deep breath, trying desperately to keep her emotions – and her powers – in check.

"Last chance," she said through gritted teeth. "Back off."

"Such a feisty one," the man taunted, his eyes raking over Jess' body in a way that made her skin crawl. "I like it."

With a glare of certainty, the man silently reached into his jacket pocket and pulled out a switchblade. Jess was horrified as she watched the knife snap open with a sickening click.

"You're going to come with me," he insisted as he moved closer into the boundary of Jess' personal space. "If you try to fuck me about, I won't hesitate to use this."

Jess stared at the sharp edge of the blade, her mind racing as she tried to weigh up her options. Her hands trembled, adrenaline surging through her. The electricity within pulsated like a living thing, desperate to escape. But she couldn't – shouldn't – use it. Not now. The consequences would be too dire.

"Fuck you," Jess ground out, her voice shaking. "I'm not going anywhere with you."

"Is that so?" the man asked, amusement lacing his words. "Well then, I guess we'll just have to do this the hard way."

He lunged at Jess, his knife slicing through the air towards her. In a state of shock, she froze on the spot. In mere seconds, he was pressing the cold steel of the blade up close to her throat.

Angry at the world, and livid at the man's gall, something suddenly snapped inside Jess. She realised that there was no other way out. This man would kill her if she didn't act now.

Instinct took over, and before she knew what was happening, she grabbed his wrist. She felt the power within her crashing to the surface like a tidal wave. She couldn't stop it. She couldn't hold it back.

A violent torrent of electricity exploded from her fingertips. It travelled up the man's arm and engulfed him in a blinding flash of blue light. He screamed and convulsed, the knife falling from his lifeless fingers as he dropped to the ground, smoke rising from his charred body.

Jess stood there in shock, her hands still tingling from the after-effects of her unleashed power. She knew she should feel remorse for what she'd done, but all she could feel was relief.

"Shit!" she said through gritted teeth.

As she stared at the man's smoking corpse, in place of the rage that had fuelled her, was now a cold, gnawing fear. She had used her powers, and there was no turning back.

Chapter Three

J ess panicked as she spotted the bus idling at the stop, its engine rumbling like a predator ready to pounce. Knowing that it was her last chance to escape the streets, she sprinted towards it.

She had to dig deep to overcome the pain that pulsed through her body with each stride. She could feel the electricity coursing through her veins, a menace threatening to break free as her fingers twitched involuntarily.

"Hey! Wait!" she called out to the driver, her voice cracking from exhaustion.

The bus was already beginning to pull away from the curb, but the driver must have caught a glimpse of Jess' desperation in the rear-view mirror. The gears screeched as the vehicle slowed.

"Thank fuck," Jess whispered, relief washing over her in waves.

She stumbled onto the bus, barely able to catch herself on the railings as she scrambled to show the driver her ticket. As the doors hissed and closed behind her, she scanned the seats quickly, looking for an empty space where she could hide and steady her shuddering hands.

She awkwardly made her way down the aisle, refusing to meet the gazes of the other passengers. It wasn't just her imagination – she could feel their stares, burning into her like hot coals as she slumped into an empty seat near the back.

Come on, she thought, willing the bus to move. *Just get me the hell out of here.*

As the bus lurched forward, she let out a shaky breath.

Ok, get it together, she told herself, fighting to stop the tears in her eyes from spilling over.

"Rough night?" a woman across the aisle asked, concern lacing her words.

Jess glanced at her, taking in the sympathetic expression on her face. Or was it pity? Or perhaps even something more sinister – like the curiosity of someone who had just witnessed a paranormal in action?

Jess' fingers twitched uncontrollably as the electricity within her begged for release. She clasped her hands together, willing them to be still.

"Something like that," she replied tersely. "I just need to get home."

"Understood," the woman said, turning her attention back to the window.

Exhausted, Jess allowed herself to sink further into the worn fabric of the bus seat. All she wanted now was to be home, cocooned beneath layers of blankets and the false sense of security they provided. Sleep beckoned like a sanctuary, promising an escape from the chaos of emotions swirling within her.

She couldn't shake the gnawing feeling that she'd been seen using her powers. The city's hatred towards paranormals was no secret. Any number of people could have seen her back there and reported her.

Please, she prayed. *Just let me get home without any more trouble.*

As she stared out of the window, watching the dark streets pass by in a blur, Jess couldn't let go of the feeling that someone was watching her. She glanced around, but all she could see was the tired faces and blank expressions of other passengers lost in their own worlds.

Maybe I'm just being paranoid, she told herself, swallowing the lump in her throat.

As the bus approached her stop and slowed to a halt, Jess braced herself for the brisk night air, pulling her jacket tighter around her slender frame. She hoped the darkness would hide any lingering traces of the panic that clung to her like a second skin.

"Thanks for the ride," she called out to the bus driver as she descended the steps.

The bus driver grunted and gave a nod before turning his attention to the road ahead.

Even though her insides were still a tangled

mess of alarm and uncertainty, Jess needed to appear normal. Trying her best to steady her nerves, she stepped out onto the pavement, inhaling deeply as she began her final stretch towards home.

With every step she took, her exhaustion threatened to overwhelm her, but she knew she couldn't let her guard down, not even for a moment. Danger could be lurking around any corner, waiting to pounce the second she showed weakness. It was that very paranoia that kept her moving, putting one foot in front of the other despite the bone-deep fatigue.

As she rounded another corner, her apartment building finally came into view – a shabby, crumbling structure that seemed to sag beneath the weight of its own decay. The sight should've been depressing, but Jess felt a spark of hope ignite within her. She was so close now; so close to the relief that awaited her within those cracked walls.

"Home sweet home," she murmured with weary sarcasm. "Never thought I'd be so damn glad to see this dump."

As she approached the apartment building's

door, she caught sight of her elderly neighbour, Mrs Wu, who was also making her way towards the entrance, albeit at a slower pace.

"Evening, Jess," Mrs Wu called out, her voice frail but sweet. "Fancy seeing you out here at this hour."

"Hey, Mrs Wu," Jess replied, forcing a smile. "Yeah, I just needed some fresh air, you know?"

"Good for you, dear," the old woman said. "It's important to take care of yourself."

Jess watched as Mrs Wu fumbled with her keys, her bun of grey hair bobbing on top of her head. Noticing that the woman was shaking slightly, Jess hesitated for a moment before stepping forward to help.

"Here, let me get the door for you," she said.

"Thank you, dear," Mrs Wu said gratefully, handing over the keys.

As Jess unlocked the door, she couldn't help but think about how vulnerable her elderly neighbour was – and how much more vulnerable she herself felt in her current state.

"You're welcome," Jess said, holding the door open for her. "You have a good night, alright?"

"Same to you, dear" Mrs Wu replied, patting Jess' arm gently before hobbling down the hallway.

As Jess stepped into the building and let the door close behind her, she still felt tense. After everything that had happened, and with her exhaustion making it even harder to hide her true nature, she had been hoping to avoid any further interactions. The last thing she wanted to do was to inadvertently expose herself to someone who could potentially be an informant for Paranormal Control.

As she walked towards her apartment, she knew that she had to stay vigilant. No matter what, she needed to maintain the veneer of normalcy.

Almost there, she thought, her hand resting on her apartment door. *In just a moment, I'll finally be safe.*

Chapter Four

Gratefully unlocking the door of her apartment, Jess slipped inside. When she slammed the door shut behind her, the sound echoed through the empty space, making her wince. She half expected Paranormal Control officers to burst in through the windows at any moment, their boots echoing on the worn linoleum floor. Leaning back against the wall, she took slow, steadying breaths, trying to calm herself.

"Ok," she said raggedly. "I made it. I'm safe… for now."

As she turned to survey the security measures on her door, doubt gnawed at her insides. There was only a standard deadbolt and a flimsy chain lock protecting her from the outside world. Were they enough to keep her safe? Could they really keep Paranormal Control at bay?

Maybe I should get one of those fancy electronic locks, she mused, biting her lip. *Or perhaps a guard dog – a big, scary one that could tear someone's face off.*

She chuckled darkly at the thought, but quickly sobered. It wasn't funny; it was survival. In a world where paranormals were hunted down and locked away, anything less than absolute caution was a death wish.

Alright, focus, she thought. *I need to be sure that no one followed me home.*

Peeking through the blinds of the small lounge, she scanned the quiet street outside. A few cars passed by, their headlights casting shadows on the pavement, but there were no SWAT vans or Paranormal Control agents lurking. At least, not that she could see.

"Seems clear," she muttered, allowing herself a small sigh of relief. "For now."

Her hands trembled as she double-checked the deadbolt and secure chain on the window. She knew that these flimsy barriers were all that stood between her and the dangerous world outside. It was both infuriating and terrifying.

Maybe I should invest in more locks, she thought, rubbing her temples. *Or bars on the windows. Or... or something.*

Stupid, stupid, stupid! she chastised herself as she paced the confines of her small living room. *Couldn't keep your goddamn powers in check for one fucking day.*

She clenched her fists, nails digging into her palms as she attempted to anchor herself to reality. Leaning against the peeling wallpaper, she stared at the chipped ceiling above her as she ran a hand through her hair. Her eyes darted around the room, searching for some semblance of stability in the chaos that was her life. The battered couch, the flickering lamp, the pile of dishes in the sink: each object seemed to mock her, a stark reminder of her failures.

"Get it together, Jess," she muttered, shaking her head as if to dispel the haze that clouded her thoughts. "You've survived this long, haven't you? You'll figure it out."

But the nagging doubt persisted, wrapping its tendrils around her and squeezing until she felt as though she couldn't breathe.

She pushed herself off the wall and began to pace again, her footsteps echoing in the cramped space. She went into the kitchen and filled the kettle with water before setting it on the stove. Its small flame seemed like a mockery of the fire that had raged within her earlier that day. She shook her head, trying to push the memory away as she rummaged through the cupboards for her favourite mug.

The kettle whistled, and Jess poured the boiling water over a teabag, watching as the liquid turned a deep amber. A dash of milk and two sugars later, she took a long, soothing mouthful, appreciating the warmth of the comforting drink.

Deciding that she had wallowed enough for one day, Jess set her mug aside. She needed to find a way to relax and ease the dull ache in her bones. A bath – that was what she needed. A hot, steaming bath would help to calm her body as well as her mind.

Without further ado, she entered the bathroom and turned on the tap, watching as water gushed into the tub. Steam clouded the air, fogging up the mirror above the sink. She grabbed a handful of bath salts, pouring them into the water with a satisfying plop. The pleasant scent of lavender filled the room.

"Time to wash away the day's bullshit," she declared.

She peeled off her clothes and stepped into the scalding water. It burned her skin for a moment, but she found solace in the pain. As she sank into the tub, her mind wandered in yearning for a life less complex.

Forcing her thoughts away, she focused on the steamy cocoon surrounding her. She felt her muscles loosen, the tension seeping out of her body. It was a rare feeling of peace, a fleeting reprieve from the constant pressure of day-to-day life. With a sigh, she let herself sink deeper into the water, allowing the warmth to chase away her fears and doubts, if only for a little while.

With the water in the bathtub cooling down, Jess reluctantly decided that it was time to get out. She could already feel the clasp of anxiety returning, digging its unforgiving claws into her. She knew that if she was to have any chance of shutting her brain off, she would have to put up a mental barrier.

Shivering, she stepped out of the bath and wrapped a towel around herself. She then padded carefully towards her bedroom, her feet leaving wet footprints on the cold floor.

Staring blankly at the mismatched socks scattered across the bedroom floor, she was tempted to analyse every detail of the day, to replay each moment over and over in her mind until it became a sickening blur of panic and uncertainty. But she knew that would only make things worse. So instead, she slipped into her favourite pair of flannel pants and a soft, worn t-shirt, promising herself that a good night's sleep would help.

She crawled into bed, her body still heavy with exhaustion. The springs groaned in protest, and the mattress sagged beneath her weight, but she barely noticed. Her mind was already drifting, caught in the hazy space between wakefulness and sleep where dreams were still a distant promise on the horizon. She closed her eyes, allowing the darkness to envelop her like a shroud, and prayed for a few hours of respite from the chaos that had become her life.

Chapter Five

The mid-morning light crept in through the thin curtains, casting a pale glow upon the room. Jess stirred beneath the tangled sheets, her mind already racing with thoughts of the day ahead.

"Fuck," she whispered.

She pushed herself up into a sitting position, rubbing the sleep from her eyes. She was determined to face whatever the day had in store for her.

"Alright," she said. "Let's do this."

Her muscles protested as she swung her legs over the edge of the bed, but she ignored the discomfort, focusing instead on the task at hand. Although a part of her was expecting to turn up at work only to be sent home, the last she knew of it, her name had been put on the rota. With a newfound optimism, she got dressed in her uniform as she prepared to make her way to the restaurant for the lunchtime shift.

***

Jess' heart raced as she manoeuvred through the crowded restaurant, her arms laden with a precariously balanced stack of dirty plates. She couldn't mess this up, not after having been sent home early from her previous shift.

A bead of sweat trickled down her temple, threatening to drip into her eye and further blur her vision. The din of clattering silverware and boisterous laughter filled her ears.

"Hey, watch where you're going!" Adele snapped.

Having narrowly avoided a collision, Jess mumbled an apology under her breath, acutely aware of the eyes that followed her every move. To these people, she was just a clumsy girl trying not to drop a stack of plates; they had no idea what she was truly capable of – or what she was hiding.

The weight of the dirty plates in her unsteady hands seemed to grow heavier by the minute, but she knew it wasn't just the physical strain causing her anxiety. It was the constant threat of being found out, of having her carefully constructed facade ripped away to reveal the extraordinary powers that lurked beneath.

Jess willed herself to keep going. Her limbs felt like lead, but she forced them to carry her forward, past tables of oblivious patrons and judgmental co-workers.

When she finally reached the relative safety of the kitchen, Jess exhaled a shaky breath. Relieved to be free of the pile of plates as she placed them in the sink, she quickly went to grab two plates of steak to take out to a table in waiting.

Weaving her way through the bustling dining area, she couldn't help but overhear part of a conversation between two customers.

"Did you hear?" said a sharply-dressed man. "There's been a murder just around the corner from here."

"Really?" said his female companion. "That's

terrible. I'm willing to bet any money that one of those god-awful paranormals is behind it. Get them all out of the city and lock them up, the lot of them!"

Fuck, Jess thought, her breath hitching. *What if they find out? What if they know it's me?*

"Here you go," she said with a forced smile as she placed the plates in front of the hungry patrons.

Their eyes grazed over her without recognition, their minds consumed by their own conversations and concerns.

"Thank you," one of them mumbled absentmindedly before diving into his meal.

Jess nodded and retreated back towards the kitchen. Her mind thrummed with thoughts of the murder, and with the terrifying possibility that her secret could be exposed.

"Jess?" the duty manager's voice cut through her thoughts like a blade, dragging her back to reality. "Can you grab more napkins from the back?"

"Sure thing," she said, trying to sound casual.

She threaded her way through the crowded restaurant and stepped into the storeroom. The door swung shut behind her, muffling the noise from the dining area. The sudden quiet was almost unnerving, a stark contrast to the clamour just beyond the thin wooden wall. It was still a welcome reprieve though; a moment of solitude in which she could gather her thoughts and steady her fraying nerves.

Her fingers grazed the rough texture of the napkins as she scooped them into her arms, the coarse fibres scraping against her skin. It was a small, grounding sensation – a reminder that she was still in the moment, despite the storm of uncertainty that swirled within her.

I wish I could leave this place forever, she thought. *Move to a new city – or maybe even the country – and start a new life. The longer I stay here, the more likely I am to be found out.*

Sighing heavily and taking the napkins into the kitchen, Jess grabbed another set of plates to take out into the dining area.

"Ah, finally," said an older woman as Jess

approached.

Jess forced a smile she didn't feel. As the woman reached out to grab the plate, her arm extended to reveal gaudy gold bracelets that jangled obnoxiously with every movement.

"Sorry for the wait, Madam," Jess said with false sincerity.

The wealthy patron barely glanced at Jess before turning her attention back to the gaggle of equally pretentious friends surrounding her.

As Jess reached down to refill their water glasses, her eyes caught sight of a sparkling diamond ring that had carelessly been placed on the edge of the table. Momentarily forgotten about in the midst of the owner's cruel gossip, it glinted in the light. To Jess, it signified a beacon of hope amidst the chaos.

Fuck it, she thought as her fingers moved at lightning-fast speed to close around the expensive piece of jewellery. These people probably had several pieces of similar jewellery stashed away somewhere at home. They surely had money to burn and seemed far too self-absorbed to have time for sentimentality.

Tucking the ring securely into her apron pocket, Jess couldn't deny her excitement. The diamond would bring exactly the kind of money she would need in order to escape this miserable existence and start anew.

"Is there anything else I can get for you?" Jess asked sweetly, her voice dripping with saccharine insincerity as she straightened up.

"Actually, there is," the woman drawled, her eyes narrowing as they flickered down to hone in on Jess' pocket. "I seem to have misplaced my ring."

"Really?" said Jess, feigning surprise as she dared to meet the woman's gaze. "That's a shame."

"Indeed," the woman replied, her lips curling into a cruel smile as though she knew exactly what Jess had done, but wanted to watch her squirm. "You should keep an eye out for it, hmm?"

"Of course," Jess said with overzealous certainty.

Turning on her heel and stalking away from the

table before she could lose control entirely, Jess navigated the busy restaurant floor, her mind buzzing with plans for her escape. She'd pawn the ring and buy a bus ticket to somewhere far away. Maybe she'd even find a place where paranormals weren't condemned and hunted. A place where she could finally belong.

Taking some deep breaths and trying to still the storm within her, Jess reasoned that she couldn't just walk out partway through her shift. It would look far too suspicious.

The ice clinked against the glass as Jess poured another round of drinks for one of the quieter tables. She couldn't shake the feeling that she was being watched, her neck prickling with unease. She glanced around the room, trying to find the source of her discomfort.

"Excuse me," a smooth voice interrupted her thoughts. "I believe we have a problem."

Jess' senses heightened as she found herself face-to-face with a tall man in an expensive suit. It was the gaudy-bracelet-wearing woman's friend.

"Problem?" Jess stuttered, trying to sound

nonchalant despite the quiver in her voice. "Is there something wrong with your order?"

"No, not with the order," the man replied, his gaze piercing through her like a knife. "But I saw you take my friend's ring. You didn't think we'd notice, did you?"

Her throat dry and her pulse throbbing in her ears, Jess felt a surge of panic – the kind that left her breathless and shaking. She couldn't lose this chance of escape, not now.

"I don't know what you're talking about," she said, her tone laced with desperation.

She could feel the power within her beginning to stir, responding to her fear and anger like a feral animal sensing blood.

"Give it back, and perhaps we can then forget that anything ever happened," the man said coolly, folding his arms across his chest.

"Fuck you," Jess said bitterly, her breath coming in short, ragged gasps. "I don't have your precious ring."

She could taste bile at the back of her throat, her

entire body thrumming with the effort it took to hold back the storm raging within. As the man's eyes widened in shock, she could see the other servers watching the confrontation with a mixture of concern and glee.

"Give it back, or I'll call the police," he threatened, his voice low and dangerous.

"Go ahead and call them," Jess shot back. "See if I care."

Her vision blurring as the power surged through her veins, she felt as though she was standing on the edge of a precipice, teetering between sanity and madness.

"Fine," the man said, pulling out his phone. "Have it your way."

As he dialled, Jess clenched her fists, feeling the heat of her power rising up inside her like a tidal wave. She tried to push it down, to keep it contained, but it was no use. It was as if the dam had finally cracked, and now there was nothing she could do to stop the flood that threatened to drown her whole.

"Please," she whispered, her voice barely

audible. "Please, don't do this."

But it was too late. The call had already been made.

The room was a cacophony of noise and chaos, but Jess only heard the roaring in her ears as her powers spiralled out of control. Her eyes blazed with an intensity that she could not contain, and the air around her seemed to crackle with energy.

The tables closest to Jess began to tremble, the silverware rattling violently on the tablecloths. The glasses began to shake, and then, as though an invisible hand had crushed them, they shattered into a thousand glittering fragments. Jess' power surged through her like wildfire, ripping through the room and causing havoc in its wake.

"Call Paranormal Control!" a young woman cried out, her eyes wide with terror. "Call them now!"

"Shut up," Jess muttered under her breath, trying desperately to rein in her powers. "Just shut up."

It was too late. The front door of the restaurant flew open with a bang, and a squad of Paranormal Control officers flooded into the room. Dressed in their distinctive black uniforms, their faces were hidden behind visors. They moved with a precision that left no doubt as to their purpose.

"Everyone down on the ground!" one of them barked. "Now!"

The restaurant patrons and staff scrambled to comply, their faces pale and their eyes wide with terror. Jess felt a wave of despair wash over her as she realised that there was no way out – she had brought this on herself.

"You're under arrest," one of the uniformed men said to her, his voice cold and emotionless. "Do not resist."

"Fuck you," Jess shouted as she spat at his feet, her powers surging with renewed strength.

She didn't care that she couldn't take them all on. She wasn't willing to go down without a fight.

"Surrender now, or we'll use force," the man

shouted.

"Fine," said Jess, too resigned to care anymore. "Do your worst."

"Take her down!" the leader barked urgently.

Jess' heart pounded in her chest. She moved swiftly, dodging the officers' attempts to subdue her.

"You'll never take me alive, you bastards!" she shouted.

Deep down, a small voice whispered to her that she couldn't keep this up forever.

"Enough!" the leader roared.

Suddenly, Jess felt the jolt of a sharp sting in her upper arm. She quickly looked down to see a dart sticking out of the muscle. The numbing effect of what she could only assume was a tranquilliser began to spread rapidly throughout her body. She felt her knees buckle and her vision blur as she collapsed onto the floor, her body betraying her.

"Target neutralised," an officer announced, his

voice devoid of compassion as he stood over Jess' limp form.

"Restrain her and let's go," the leader ordered.

Jess felt strong hands gripping her arms as her wrists were bound together behind her back. She tried to resist the encroaching blackness, to summon another surge of power – anything to escape this nightmare – but her body refused to respond.

"Please…" she whispered.

Her plea went unheard as the world faded away, leaving her trapped in darkness and defeat.

Chapter Six

Jess' eyelids fluttered open, her vision blurred and unfocused. Her head ached, throbbing with every beat of her pulse. She tried to remember what had happened, but her thoughts were scrambled and incoherent.

"Where... where am I?" she mumbled, her voice ringing in her ears.

She attempted to move, but her limbs felt like lead weights, unresponsive and heavy. As she struggled on the unfamiliar bed, her body sluggish and uncooperative, panic began to rise in her chest.

"Come on, damn it," she muttered, frustration boiling inside her.

Memories of shouts and screams from customers in the restaurant flickered at the edge of her mind, teasing her with snippets of information that refused to come together into a cohesive picture. She knew something was wrong – very wrong – but couldn't put her finger on it.

When she finally managed to prop herself up on her elbows, her confusion gave way to fear, gnawing at her insides like a ravenous beast.

"Ok," she whispered, her voice shaky but resolute. "You need to figure out what the hell is going on."

Her thoughts churned, searching for answers to her predicament. She strained against the fog clouding her mind, desperate to piece together the fragments of her memory.

"Tranquilliser... someone shot me with a tranquilliser..."

As soon as the words had tumbled from her lips, the memory grew clearer. The realisation caused her to shudder.

She blinked, her vision sharpening as she focused on the sterile environment around her. The pristine white walls seemed to gleam in the dim light, and the minimalist furnishings only heightened the sense of isolation and coldness that enveloped her.

"Where the fuck am I?" she said under her breath.

She swung her legs over the edge of the bed, her muscles protesting at the sudden movement. With gritted teeth, she forced herself to stand, steadying her balance against the wall as her head swam.

"Come on, Jess," she whispered fiercely, refusing to let her body betray her. "You need answers. You can't stay here like a sitting duck."

Slowly, with each step feeling like a battle won, she made her way across the room towards the door, a feeling of dread building within her.

As she reached for the handle, something caught her eye – an emblem displayed on the door's surface. She squinted to read the writing underneath the elaborately designed crest.

Elemental Academy?! What the hell is that?! she wondered.

She didn't have to wonder for long. Hearing footsteps approaching from the corridor outside, she quickly stood back from the door. She watched tentatively as it opened and in walked a tall woman with pale skin, her hair scraped back into a ponytail. She looked to be a little younger than Jess, although certainly anything but naive.

"Who the hell are you?" Jess demanded, her voice wavering despite her best efforts to sound tough.

"Ah, apologies for the abrupt introduction," the woman said as she stepped forward, her movements fluid and graceful. "I'm Morgan. I'm one of the mentors here at Elemental Academy."

"Great," Jess muttered, her arms crossed defensively over her chest. "So why am I here?"

"Your powers, Jess," Morgan said, her voice low and enticing, as if revealing a coveted secret. "We know all about your abilities. You're special, and this academy is where you belong."

"How do you know about my powers?" Jess quizzed, her eyes narrowing and her suspicion flaring. "Who's been watching me?"

A feeling of vulnerability gnawed at her insides as she realised that someone must have been monitoring her.

"Many eyes have been on you, Jess," Morgan said cryptically. "But we are not here to harm you – quite the opposite, in fact. We want to help you learn to control your abilities, and for you to understand their true potential."

"Control them?" Jess scoffed. "I've been doing just fine on my own, thank you very much."

"Really?" Morgan asked in a challenging tone with one brow raised. "Tell me, Jess, have you ever felt at ease with the full extent of your power? In control of the raw energy coursing through your veins, begging to be unleashed?"

The question caught Jess off guard. Her mind raced with memories of countless moments where her powers had threatened to spiral out of control. In the darkest recesses of her mind, she knew Morgan was right: she had never truly managed to control her abilities.

Jess shyly turned her attention to the tiles

beneath her feet. She couldn't quite look Morgan in the eye.

"Here at the academy, you can learn to harness your power and transform it into something extraordinary," said Morgan, her eyes gleaming with intensity, as though she could see into the very core of Jess' soul. "But first, you must let go of your worries and doubts."

"That's easy for you to say," Jess grumbled, her thoughts a chaotic whirlwind of emotions.

Deep down, she was struggling to conceal her curiosity. However, having experienced so much disappointment in her life, she couldn't allow herself to get carried away. The mere suggestion that there were people out there who could help her understand and control her powers wasn't something to be taken lightly.

"There are others here who understand your struggles," Morgan said, her voice cutting through Jess' thoughts. "Come with me, I'll introduce you to some of the other students here."

Jess nodded, her throat dry. She followed Morgan down a narrow corridor. The walls were adorned with framed portraits of, presumably, paranormals of note. Jess couldn't help but wonder what they knew that she didn't, and if they too had grappled with the same challenges.

"Here we are," Morgan announced as she pushed open a set of double doors.

Before them was a spacious lounge. It was filled with clusters of mismatched sofas and armchairs. A group of people – all in the same uniform as Morgan and all probably in their twenties – lounged about, engrossed in conversation or buried in books.

"Everyone, this is Jess," Morgan called out, catching the occupants' attention.

"Hi Jess!" a girl with fiery red hair said, beaming as she hopped up from her seat. "I'm Cassie. I can manipulate fire."

Cassie snapped her fingers, causing a small flame to dance above her thumb.

"Nice to meet you," Jess replied hesitantly, eyeing the flame with a mixture of admiration and caution.

"Hey, I'm Leo," a lanky guy with glasses called out, extending his hand in greeting. "I can move things with my mind."

As if to prove his point, he levitated a pencil from a nearby table, making it twirl in midair.

"Wow," said Jess, her eyes following the pencil's path. "That's... impressive."

"Jess can manipulate electricity," Morgan explained.

"Something like that," Jess said warily, not quite sure of how best to describe her powers.

"That's fantastic!" said Cassie, clapping her hands together in delight. "You'll fit right in."

"Maybe," Jess said quietly, not quite convinced.

She just couldn't shake the feeling that she was an outsider. Long ago, she had come to accept it as fact.

"Is it always like this?" she asked, casting a cynical eye over the diverse group. "Everyone just... showing off their powers?"

"Sometimes," Leo admitted, shrugging. "But most of the time, we're just trying to figure out how to make the best of them, you know? This is the only place where we can be ourselves without apology."

"Exactly," Cassie chimed in. "Out there, in the world beyond the academy, we have to hide who we are. Here, we can embrace it."

Jess watched the students, awed by their control over their powers, but also deeply unsettled. Feeling like an impostor among the truly gifted, she wasn't sure that she belonged here.

"What if I can't do it?" she blurted out, her voice trembling with fear and frustration. "What if I can never figure out how to control my powers?"

"Jess," Morgan replied gently, placing a reassuring hand on her shoulder. "You're here because the academy wants to help you. Not only that, but they see potential in you. They believe you can learn, just like the rest of us."

"Besides," Cassie added. "You've already shown that you have power. You just need to learn how to harness it."

"How can you all be so sure?" Jess demanded.

"Your question is valid," Morgan confirmed, her expression unreadable. "But I can assure you that the academy's intentions are noble. They've brought us here not to exploit us, but to help us thrive in a world that fears us."

"Listen, Jess," Leo said earnestly, his brow furrowed in concern. "We get that you're scared. We all were at first. But this place, these people – they're on our side. And the sooner you accept that, the sooner you can really start living."

Jess looked from Leo to Morgan and Cassie, their faces filled with sincerity and conviction. She wanted to believe them, to trust in the promise of this strange new world, but doubt still gnawed at her, threatening to tear her apart.

"Listen," said Morgan, her tone gentle having sensed Jess' turmoil. "If you wish to join us here at Elemental Academy, there's a place for you. You don't have to accept it; it's entirely up to you. But something tells me that you haven't been coping too well on the outside."

"I..." Jess began, ready to defend herself.

"You don't have to give us an answer now," Morgan assured, her voice sweet and soothing. "Let's get you settled for the night. Sleep on it, and if you're ready to, get back to us with an answer in the morning."

Morgan gestured for Jess to follow her out of the room. As they walked through the pristine halls of the academy, Jess couldn't help but feel like an intruder – a wild, unpredictable anomaly that threatened to disrupt the order and stability that this place represented.

Eventually, they reached an empty dormitory room.

"Make yourself at home," said Morgan. "I'll leave you to it for now. I'm sure you've had quite a day."

As the enigmatic young woman closed the door behind her, Jess sank onto the bed, her head spinning with thoughts of the outside world – of the people who had looked at her with horror and disgust when her powers had been exposed, of the isolation that had gnawed at her every day. Her fingers traced the smooth, cool bed sheets as she fought back tears. This place, this Elemental Academy, was supposed to be her salvation. But why did it feel like a prison?

She wanted more than anything to phone Tom and to let him know where she was, but where could she possibly start? Besides, she had no idea where her phone was – as far as she could recall, it wasn't on her person when she'd woken up bleary-eyed in that strange white room.

"Fuck," she muttered, swiping angrily at the tears that betrayed her.

She knew in all honesty, that staying here was her only option. The outside world was no place for people like her – those who were different, those who wielded powers they couldn't control. With each incident that had left her feeling more broken and alone than before, Jess couldn't hide from the fact that she needed help.

With a heavy sigh and a lingering sense of unease, she resigned herself to the truth: she would have to stay at the academy. For better or for worse, this could be her only chance to finally gain control of her powers, and to find her place in the cruel, paranormal-hating outside world. Although she wasn't quite sure of how she had ended up in that white room, and although she didn't really have much choice, perhaps the strange olive branch that had been put within her already-defeated grasp was all she had left.

Chapter Seven

The first beams of sunlight crept into the bedroom, casting a warm glow across Jess' face as she stirred from her slumber. She opened her eyes, blinking away the lingering remnants of sleep as she stretched.

The unfamiliarity of the room struck her for a moment, but the realisation of where she was soon flooded back. This was it: her chance for a better life, a place where she could learn to control her powers and be accepted for who she was. A sense of determination welled up within her, and she knew that she had made the right decision.

Alright, she thought, steeling her nerves. *This is your chance. Make it count.*

She swung her legs over the side of the bed, her feet connecting with the cool floor. She glanced down at her work clothes, and cringed; they were still crumpled and stained from the day before. They wouldn't make for the best first impression, but they would have to do for now. As she stood up, she felt the weight of uncertainty in her gut, but refused to let it overpower her newfound resolve.

Fuck it, she thought, running her fingers through her tousled hair in an attempt to tame it. *I've dealt with worse.*

She stepped towards the small mirror hanging on the wall, examining her reflection. There were dark circles under her eyes, a testament to the restless nights spent grappling with the reality of her situation. Despite her dishevelled appearance though, there was a fire in her eyes. It emanated a sense of purpose that burned bright against the shadows of her past.

"Today's the day," she said, her voice steady as she locked eyes with her reflection. "No more hiding. No more running."

Taking a deep breath to centre herself, Jess prepared to leave the sanctuary of the humble bedroom to face the world beyond its walls. She was consumed by a whirlwind of anticipation, her emotions swirling.

She stepped quietly out of her room, her eyes scanning the hallway for any sign of Morgan. Although Jess was reluctant to trust anyone, she couldn't deny that Morgan had been a welcome anchor amongst the chaos that had surrounded her arrival at the academy.

Taking a few cautious steps down the hall, Jess felt a wave of relief wash over her as soon as she spotted Morgan, who offered a warm and reassuring smile.

"Hey, there you are!" Morgan called out, her eyes locking onto Jess. "I was just coming to check on you."

"Perfect timing," Jess replied. "Morgan, I've made up my mind."

Maintaining her supportive demeanour, Morgan tilted her head curiously.

"I want to stay here and learn how to control my powers," Jess said with fierce conviction. "I want to be a part of this place, to become something more than just... this."

She gestured at the crumpled work clothes that clung to her body, a reminder of the life she was mostly looking forward to leaving behind.

"I'm so glad to hear that," said Morgan, her eyes sparkling with understanding. "You're making the right choice, Jess. This place can really change your life if you let it."

"I hope so," Jess mused. "So... what's next?"

"First of all, we need to get you officially enrolled," Morgan said, signalling for Jess to follow her.

As they walked side by side, their footsteps echoing in the bustling corridors of the academy, a vibrant energy filled the air. The atmosphere was alive with the sights and sounds of students immersed in their extraordinary pursuits. Jess' eyes widened as she witnessed a kaleidoscope of captivating scenes unfolding before her.

Everywhere she looked, students exhibited their supernatural abilities, creating a mesmerising spectacle. In one corner, a group of students levitated objects with effortless grace, demonstrating their telekinetic prowess. Nearby, a pair engaged in a friendly sparring session, their bodies surrounded by swirling elemental energies. The crackle of lightning and the whoosh of wind served to emphasise the participants' mastery.

In another hallway, a student manipulated the very fabric of reality, warping time and space with a wave of their hand. The resulting distortions created a visually stunning display that left Jess awestruck. Each student she encountered seemed to possess a unique gift, a remarkable power that set them apart from the ordinary world.

It wasn't just the displays of raw power that fascinated Jess. Each of the academy's corridors were abuzz with a vibrant blend of activity. Groups of students gathered in animated discussions, exchanging knowledge and experiences. In one corner, a study circle sat engrossed in ancient tomes and arcane texts, their curiosity driving them to unlock the mysteries of their abilities.

Laughter and friendly banter filled the air as friendships formed and bonds strengthened. Jess couldn't help but feel a sense of camaraderie and belonging as she observed the students' interactions. The academy was evidently a place where they could be their authentic selves, free from the burden of having to hide their powers. Here, their extraordinary nature was celebrated and nurtured. It was a far cry from the life she had become so accustomed to in the unforgiving city back home, which seemed almost cruel by comparison.

For the first time in her life, Jess dared to believe that maybe, just maybe, she was finally where she belonged. She had spent so much of her life feeling like an outsider, an anomaly in a world that sought to suppress and control people like her. But now, as she walked through the heart of the academy, she was almost beginning to feel at home.

"Wow!" she exclaimed, her eyes wide with wonder. "I can't believe this place."

"Believe it," Morgan said with a friendly chuckle.

"Thanks," said Jess, excited to know more. "So, what kind of classes do we take here? I mean, I know we must learn to control our powers, but... you know?"

"Good question," said Morgan, guiding Jess

around a corner. "We have a mixture of practical and theoretical courses. Some classes place emphasis on showing us how to hone our powers, whilst others are designed to teach us about the history and ethics of paranormals in society. Professor Kaplan is especially knowledgeable in that area."

"Professor Kaplan?" Jess repeated, her interest piqued.

"Right," Morgan confirmed. "He's the head professor here. He's got quite a reputation for helping students reach their full potential."

Jess furrowed her brow, making a mental note to remember the information for future reference.

They continued down another hallway, passing more students engaged in various activities. Jess found herself marvelling at their seemingly effortless control over their powers. She couldn't help but wonder how long it would take for her to attain the same level of mastery.

"Hey, don't worry," Morgan said, as if having read Jess' thoughts. "We all start somewhere, right? The important thing is that you're here now, ready to learn and grow."

As they approached the door to Professor Kaplan's office, Jess took one last look around the bustling hallways, unable to deny her fascination.

"Here we are," said Morgan, her voice full of quiet confidence as she gestured to the door. "Remember, Professor Kaplan is on your side. He wants to help you succeed."

Jess nodded, bracing herself as she prepared to knock on the door. Her hand shook slightly, but she was determined not to let her nerves get the better of her. With a final glance at Morgan, she wrapped her knuckles against the elegantly-designed wood.

"Come in," called a vibrant voice from within the room.

Easing the door open, Jess anxiously stepped into the office. The room was bathed in a golden light that filtered in through the tall windows lining one of the walls. The other walls were adorned with shelves full of academic memorabilia – from neatly stacked piles of papers and books, to trophies, medals and certificates of achievement.

There was a large mahogany desk at the far side of the cedarwood-scented room. From behind it, a distinguished man with silver hair and wide-rimmed glasses stood up to greet Jess with a reassuring smile. Appearing to be in his fifties, he had kind eyes that held the promise of experience, intelligence, and warmth.

"Welcome to Elemental Academy," he greeted, extending a hand for Jess to shake. "I trust that you've come to see me because you wish to enrol?"

"Yes, Sir. Thank you, Sir," Jess replied, feeling a surge of pride as she shook his hand.

She marvelled at how different their interaction felt in comparison to her past experiences with authority figures, who often regarded her with disdain. Unlike in those instances, Professor Kaplan seemed genuinely pleased to be talking to her.

"Please, have a seat," he said as he gestured towards a comfortable-looking chair across from his desk.

As Jess sat down, she couldn't help but feel impressed.

"Before we begin the enrolment process, I want to make sure you understand that Elemental Academy is not just about honing your abilities," Professor Kaplan emphasised. "It's also about learning to use them responsibly."

Like when I killed that man the other night! Fuck! Jess chastised herself. *Yeah, sure, Jess, that was really responsible, wasn't it!*

Trying to silence the remnants of guilt that had brutally just cropped up in her mind, Jess nodded, her thoughts racing. She knew that the academy was her chance to prove herself and to finally embrace her true potential, regardless of what had happened.

"Of course, Sir," she replied, determination filling her voice. "I'm ready to do whatever it takes."

"Excellent," Professor Kaplan said, his eyes twinkling with approval. "Now, let's get started."

He pulled open a drawer and produced a stack

of papers, each neatly clipped together.

"These documents outline the academy's policies, our academic expectations, and the resources available to you during your time here," he said. "I'll go through them with you, and if you're in agreement, you can sign at the bottom of each page."

He began explaining the first document, which focused on the academy's code of conduct. Jess listened intently as he detailed the importance of respecting fellow students, instructors, and staff members, along with maintaining high ethical standards in the use of supernatural powers.

"Remember," he said, tapping the paper for emphasis. "The choices you make here will not just impact your own life, but the lives of all those around you."

Jess nodded solemnly. After what she had done back in the city, she couldn't help but feel that in signing the documents, she was being a hypocrite.

How long are you going to beat yourself up over this shit?! she told herself. *Start looking to the future, Jess!*

With the thrum of electricity throbbing beneath her skin, and with a trembling hand, she signed her name.

"We're almost done now," Professor Kaplan said. "Make good use of the resources we have available to support your development. Our library holds countless tomes on paranormal studies – from historical records to theoretical treatises. We also have state-of-the-art facilities for physical training, meditation, and elemental control. It's imperative, however, for you to recognise that the most critical resource you possess is within yourself: your own determination and willingness to grow."

"Yes, Sir," Jess said with a nod as she took in the professor's serious expression.

"And remember," he added, leaning forward and intently meeting Jess' gaze. "You are not defined solely by your abilities, but by how you choose to wield them. Embrace this journey, Jess, and never forget that the potential for greatness resides in all of us."

Humbly gripping her fingers around the pen,

Jess finished signing the remaining documents. A sense of pride and commitment washed over her as the reality hit home: she was now officially a student of Elemental Academy.

85

Chapter Eight

Jess inhaled deeply as she stepped into the classroom, her chest tightening with anticipation as she glanced around at all the students. She scanned the room, taking note of the various expressions on their faces – some were wide-eyed with curiosity, whilst others seemed more relaxed.

Not quite sure what to expect, Jess made her way to an empty seat.

"Attention, everyone!" announced a commanding voice.

Jess looked up to observe the man who had just instantly silenced the room. He strode to the front of the class. His presence was undeniably captivating, his silver hair and piercing blue eyes only adding to his distinguished appearance. He exuded an aura of authority that demanded respect. Jess felt a combination of admiration and excitement bubble up within her as she prepared to hear his words.

"Good morning, everyone," he said. "Ah, Jess, I understand that you're new here. I'm Professor Schrager. You're going to be with me for your Paranormal Concepts course. Everyone has to take this class, regardless of what their specific powers are."

Jess nodded diligently, too impressed to speak. It wasn't often that she was lost for words.

"Now then," Professor Schrager continued. "I'm sure many of you have questions – about your powers, about your purpose, about what it means to be a paranormal. I encourage you to ask those questions, to challenge the assumptions and myths that pervade our society."

"Professor," a young woman called out from the back of the class. "What do you mean by 'challenge the assumptions'? Surely it's a given that we're not the same as normal people?"

A hush fell over the room as everyone awaited Professor Schrager's response.

"An excellent question," he answered brightly. "Yes, we are different from those without elemental abilities, but that does not make us superior, nor does it entitle us to treat others with anything less than respect and dignity."

"Damn right," someone else muttered under their breath, earning a few murmurs of agreement from the students around them.

"Furthermore, our powers do not define us, nor should they dictate our sense of self-worth," Professor Schrager continued. "We are all complex individuals who possess unique strengths and weaknesses – both within and beyond the scope of our supernatural abilities."

Jess felt a spark of hope ignite within her as the professor's words echoed around the room. For years, she had been tormented by the notion that her powers made her a freak, an outcast from the society that she so desperately wanted to belong to. But now, here was someone – an esteemed professor, no less – telling her that she was more than just the taboo of her abilities.

"Remember," said Professor Schrager, his voice taking on a solemn note. "Elemental Academy exists to guide and support you on your journey towards understanding and harnessing your powers for good. It's up to you to embrace this opportunity and strive for growth – both as paranormals and as human beings."

Hanging on the professor's every word, Jess sat up higher in her seat.

"Before we delve into our specific elements, we must first understand what it means to be a paranormal," Professor Schrager said, his eyes sweeping over the class. "You are all individuals with inherent powers over a particular element. Be it fire, water, earth, air, or something else entirely. Each of you possesses an innate connection to one or more of the vital forces around you."

A murmur of intrigue rippled through the room as some of the students exchanged glances, several eager to share their own elemental affiliations. Jess remained silent, her thoughts focused on her unique connection to electricity. It felt surreal to be surrounded by paranormals who felt no shame in announcing their powers. The shame had been a particularly crippling burden for her.

"Many people assume that these powers are

hereditary," Professor Schrager said, silencing the whispers with a raised hand. "That they're passed on through the bloodlines from one generation to the next. However, this is not necessarily the case. Whilst it's true that elemental abilities can run in families, there are countless examples of paranormals with no known relatives who share their powers."

Jess felt mostly relieved to hear this. She hated the thought of Tom having to go through some of the things she'd been through.

"In fact, evidence suggests that the origin of our powers might be far more mysterious – perhaps even divine in nature," said the professor.

"Divine?" Jess mused.

The word had slipped out before she could stop it. The idea that her powers could be the result of something otherworldly, rather than a genetic quirk, was both thrilling and terrifying.

"Indeed," Professor Schrager replied, his eyes meeting Jess' with a knowing smile. "There is still so much that we don't understand about the origins of our abilities, but it's important to keep an open mind as we explore these mysteries."

Jess nodded, her thoughts racing with possibilities. She had always believed that her powers were simply a part of who she was – like her freckles or her dark hair. But now, she couldn't help but wonder if there was more to her powers – something greater and more intense.

As Professor Schrager continued to unravel the hidden depths of what it meant to be a paranormal, Jess' eyes were locked onto his every gesture, her ears taking in his every word. A storm of questions brewed in her mind, each one more tantalising than the last.

"Whilst our powers may be extraordinary, they do not make us superior beings," the professor emphasised. "We are no better or worse than anyone else; we simply possess different abilities."

Another murmur of agreement rippled through the classroom. Jess felt proud to be part of a community that valued equality and humility. Back in the city, she had never experienced that.

"Alright, everyone," said Professor Schrager, his tone shifting to a more conversational one. "I'd like you to think about a situation where someone might have been treated unfairly due to their abilities, or lack thereof. Share your thoughts with the rest of the class."

Still ashamed of her struggles, Jess didn't feel comfortable to volunteer any information just yet. Instead, she decided that she would be best off keeping quiet about them. She doubted that anyone else had murdered someone, or even tried stealing to survive. She wanted to hear from others first. Had their lives been just as hard?

"Back in my hometown, there was this kid who could manipulate water," a young man spoke out. "People were afraid of him because they didn't understand his powers, so they shunned him and treated him terribly. But he was just as human as the rest of us."

"I can relate to that," a woman with red hair replied. "I've been treated differently because of my powers too. It's... not a great feeling."

"Exactly," another student concurred, her voice fierce with conviction. "We're all just people trying to make our way in the world."

It surprised Jess to know that in some places,

paranormals were perhaps under less pressure to hide their powers. It crossed her mind that possibly, in its employment of Paranormal Control, her city was one of the more severe places for a paranormal to live. A shiver ran down her spine as she remembered the years spent hiding her powers, cowering in the shadows of a city that sought to persecute her for being different.

Although she was still too afraid to speak out about her own experiences, Jess found herself yearning to learn more about her classmates and their unique abilities.

She stared at her hands, her fingers twitching with the barely restrained energy that coursed beneath her skin. For so long, she had believed herself to be an aberration, destined to be shunned by society. But now, sitting among others who also had extraordinary abilities, she was beginning to question her self-perception.

Fuck, she thought, a sudden realisation hitting her like a bolt of lightning. How many nights had she spent crying herself to sleep, cursing the cruel twist of fate that had bestowed upon her these unwanted powers?

Jess couldn't tear her eyes away from Professor Schrager as he continued his lecture. With his words having struck a chord deep within her, she found herself hanging onto every syllable.

Chapter Nine

The closed classroom door exploded inward with a deafening crash, splinters of wood flying through the air like shrapnel. A swarm of black-clad figures stormed into the room, weapons raised and aimed directly at Jess. The shock on her fellow students' faces mirrored her own, their eyes wide with terror as they scrambled to process the sudden intrusion.

"Jessica Winters!" barked the leader of the SWAT team, his voice cold and authoritative. "You're under arrest for the murder of Jeremy Shaw!"

Jess' heart hammered in her chest. Although she had acted in self-defence that fateful night, deep down, she had been expecting this moment to come. Now it was alarmingly clear that her actions had caught up with her, and that the consequences were about to become all too real.

Her hands shook as she raised them in the air, her throat tight with fear and shame.

"Please," she whispered, desperate for someone, anyone, to understand. "I didn't have a choice."

In the midst of the chaos, screams and shouts filled the air as students scattered in every direction, desperate to escape the armed intruders. Professor Schrager's eyes, however, remained locked on Jess, assessing her trembling frame with a mixture of concern and determination.

"Everyone stay calm!" he shouted above the din, his voice authoritative and controlled.

With a fluid motion, he stepped forward, positioning himself between the frightened students and the SWAT team. In place of his previously calm demeanour was an intense focus that cut through the pandemonium like a razor.

"Jess, don't move," he said under his breath. "I'll handle this."

Jess nodded shakily as Professor Schrager whipped out his mobile phone, his fingers flying over the screen as he dialled. When the call connected, he spoke urgently, his words laced with adrenaline.

"Professor Kaplan!" he said loud and clear. "We have a situation in my classroom! The SWAT team are here for Jess – they're accusing her of murder!"

Professor Schrager paused, listening intently to his colleague's response before continuing.

"Your assistance is needed immediately," he said. "Hurry!"

Jess' hands clenched into tight fists, her knuckles white with tension as she fought the urge to bolt, to flee from the nightmare unfolding before her.

Please, she thought, her mind racing. *Someone help me.*

As the seconds ticked away, Jess' gaze flickered between the determined face of Professor Schrager and the merciless glare of the SWAT team. A cold, heavy dread settled in the pit of her stomach as she realised that no matter what was about to happen, her life would never be the same again.

The tension in the room was palpable, an abundance of shock and looming uncertainty. Jess' breaths came in shallow gasps as she took in the standoff between her classmates and the armed intruders. She could feel the weight of the students' stares, their eyes darting between her and the SWAT team, silently pleading for answers.

Suddenly, with an air of authoritative force, Professor Kaplan strode into the room. As he surveyed the scene before him, his expression was hard and unyielding.

"Enough!" he bellowed, his voice slicing through the tension.

As one, the students and the SWAT team froze, their gazes snapping to the imposing professor.

"Now then, Commander Voss," Professor Kaplan addressed the head of the SWAT team, his tone firm and unwavering. "As I understand it, your team has been given orders to apprehend Miss Jessica Winters. However, I must insist that this young woman is given a fair trial. Elemental Academy is equipped to handle situations like this, and we will not tolerate any undue cruelty or injustice."

"Then you should damn well know that she's wanted for murder," Commander Voss said angrily, his finger twitching on the trigger of his gun. "We're taking her into custody, and that's final."

"Jess deserves a decent chance to defend herself," Professor Kaplan argued, his gaze never leaving the armed man's. "She's one of our students, and we have a duty to protect her rights. You know we've got adequate detainment facilities here."

Shit, Jess thought, her panic heightening as she listened to the negotiation unfolding before her. *What if they don't let me stay? What if they take me away?*

"Fine," Commander Voss said through gritted teeth, his eyes narrowing as he considered the professor's words. "You can keep temporary custody of Winters, but I'll be staying to oversee her confinement."

"Agreed," Professor Kaplan replied, his expression unreadable as he nodded in approval.

"Good," said Commander Voss, turning to bark orders at his team. "Get this place secured and let's get her locked up."

As the SWAT team dispersed, Jess broke out into a cold sweat. She knew that her fate was in the hands of others, and although she was grateful for Professor Kaplan's intervention, she couldn't shake the feeling that everything was about to change for the worst.

Please, she prayed silently, her eyes darting between the stern faces of the professors and the SWAT team. *Let me find a way through this.*

With her pulse racing, Jess could only watch helplessly as the SWAT team began to close in on her. She knew that her guilt was not up for debate: she had killed, even if it was in self-defence.

The cold steel of the handcuffs snapped her back to reality.

"Fuck this," she muttered under her breath.

Her eyes scanned the classroom for any possible route of escape. Her desperation clawed at her; she couldn't just stand there and let them imprison her.

"Jess, don't," Professor Schrager warned, his voice laced with concern.

"Can't you see? I have no choice!" she shot back, her voice cracking as tears threatened to spill over.

Despite the handcuffs, she forcefully yanked her body free from the grasp of one of the men.

"Stop her!" the burly man bellowed, his face contorted with rage.

The room erupted into chaos once more, students diving out of the way as Jess tried to sprint and weave her way past.

"Let me go!" she screamed. "I didn't mean to kill anyone!"

"Grab her!" Commander Voss ordered, pointing to a particularly muscular colleague.

"Please," Jess begged.

She cast a desperate glance back at Professor Kaplan, who shook his head sadly. It was clear that there was nothing more he could do for her.

"Get your hands off me!" Jess said with a snarl.

Briefly summoning her powers in a last-resort attempt to break free, she felt a jolt of electricity course through her body, but it was gone as quickly as it had arrived. She slumped forward in defeat, too overwhelmed to function.

"Jess!" Professor Schrager called out. "I promise we'll do everything in our power to help you."

"Thanks," she said weakly, not quite believing that anybody could help her now.

She turned her gaze to the floor as shame and dread filled her to the brim. She knew what she had done, acting in self-defence, but that didn't change the fact that a life had been taken by her hands. The consequences of her actions loomed over her like a dark cloud, threatening to engulf her completely.

As she was dragged from the classroom, she couldn't help but glance back at her fellow students, their eyes wide with shock and pity.

"Keep moving, Winters," Commander Voss barked, his demeanour more brutal now that they were alone in the corridor. "You're not getting any sympathy from me."

Jess clenched her jaw, her fear giving way to a surge of anger.

"I don't need your sympathy," she protested, her voice shaking with emotion. "Just tell me what's going to happen to me."

"First, you'll be taken to the academy's detention cells," he explained, his tone clinical. "Then, you'll face a tribunal of judges who will determine your fate. And I must say, your chances aren't looking too good."

"Is there anything I can do?" she asked, her mind racing through all the possible outcomes. "I didn't mean for it to happen."

"Save it for the tribunal," Commander Voss scoffed. "Your excuses won't change anything. You broke the law, and now you have to face the consequences."

As they approached the underground confinement cells, Jess couldn't help but shudder. The overwhelmingly small space was just like a dungeon, damp and reeking of mould. The flickering, muted glow from the fluorescent lights mounted upon the worn walls served to provide hardly any illumination amongst the darkness.

"Welcome to your new home," Commander Voss said with a sneer as he roughly removed Jess' handcuffs and shoved her into a cell. "I hope you find it to your liking."

"Piss off," she snapped. "Rot in hell!"

She shot him one last venomous glare before he slammed the heavy metal door shut. The sound of his thudding footsteps then faded away down the small alcove towards the exit.

Left alone in the darkness, Jess sank down to the cold, hard floor and let out a choked sob. The weight of her predicament pressed down on her chest like a slab of stone, making it hard to breathe. How had everything gone so wrong, so fast?

"Stupid," she muttered to herself, blinking back tears.

It was all her fault – every mistake, every bad decision that had led her here. And now, she'd have to pay the price for foolishly having dared to believe that she could outrun her past.

"Stupid, stupid, stupid," she whispered brokenly as the shadows closed in around her.

Chapter Ten

Jess' fingers dug into her scalp, the rhythmic scratching a desperate attempt to stave off the madness that threatened to consume her. The dank cell had become a living nightmare, its dark corners crawling with shadows and phantom whispers.

"Self-defence," she muttered, frantically clinging to that truth. "It was self-fucking-defence."

Her voice wavering, fragile and brittle, it didn't sound convincing even to her own ears. She thought of the other paranormals and of how they must see her now: a murderer, a monster they couldn't trust or respect.

"Fuck!" she shouted as the darkness seemed to inch in closer around her.

She screamed, slamming her fist against a wall. Pain shot through her hand, but it was a welcome distraction from the torment of her mind.

"Jess?" a soft voice interrupted, tentative and surprised.

It was Cassie, concern etched on her face as she peered through the opening in the cell door.

"What are you doing here?" Jess whispered, amazed and relieved to see someone other than Commander Voss.

"Hey," Cassie whispered. "I pulled some strings so I could bring you this meal. I want to talk to you."

Through the opening, Jess grabbed the tray, her fingers brushing against Cassie's for a brief moment. The contact sent a jolt of warmth through her cold and shaking hands. Almost embarrassed about her desperation for comfort, Jess stepped back and put the tray down on the makeshift bed that she'd fashioned out of the few blankets provided to her.

"What's happening up there?" she asked, her

thoughts racing as she wondered what Cassie was risking in visiting her.

"I've got news," Cassie said. "I think you'll want to hear it."

"Tell me everything," Jess pleaded.

She needed something to hold onto, any shred of hope that her life wasn't over.

"Professor Kaplan's been working non-stop on your case, Jess," Cassie said, her voice sincere. "He believes in you. He's doing everything he can to protect your freedom."

"Really?" Jess asked, disbelieving but hopeful.

"Well, he's doing everything he can, but it's not easy," Cassie admitted, her brow furrowed with worry.

"Oh," said Jess. "But hang on, what if..."

"Shit!" Cassie exclaimed in a frantic whisper. "Commander Voss is coming! I have to go!"

"Wait!..." Jess started.

It was too late. Cassie had already gone, leaving Jess alone with the burden of questions unanswered.

Jess stared at the door, overwhelmed as she tried to make sense of what Cassie had said. The thought that someone out there was even willing to fight her corner was almost intoxicating, but she couldn't shake the nagging feeling that all the same, she was still doomed.

She stared at her meal with mixed feelings, her stomach rumbling as she assessed the blue plastic plate. She wanted to eat, if only as an act of defiance to prove that she hadn't given up.

A modest portion of meat and green beans occupied the small space, their once-steaming surfaces now slick with congealed grease. It wasn't the most appetising sight, but in her predicament, Jess was in no position to complain. A pang of hunger for something better stirred within her, but she chastised herself for even allowing such thoughts.

"Could be worse," she mumbled, poking at the cold food with a plastic fork. "This is probably gourmet compared to what I'll get in prison as a convicted murderer."

She sighed, taking a hesitant bite of the meat. A greasy, stringy texture greeted her tongue and the roof of her mouth, leaving her longing for a hot meal that would never come. As she took another bite, rather than the coldness of her surroundings and the bleak future that awaited her, she tried to focus on the kindness that had been shown to her by some.

Suddenly, the sound of heavy footsteps echoed against the cold, hard floor, breaking the eerie silence that had settled over Jess' cell. With a mixture of dread and anticipation, she looked up from her spot on the floor. The footsteps grew louder, more deliberate, until the unmistakably stern features of Commander Voss appeared through the narrow opening of the cell door.

"Ah, I see you've finished your meal," he said with a sneer, his cruel eyes lingering on the tray, which had been pushed to one side. "Or at least, what you could stomach of it."

Refusing to take the bait, Jess clenched her jaw. She remained silent as she passed the tray to him through the door.

"It's such a shame this accommodation doesn't meet your standards," he continued, his voice dripping with sarcasm. "But then again, beggars – especially *murderers* – can't be choosers."

"Fuck you," said Jess, the thrum of electric rage coursing through her veins.

"Watch your tongue, girl!" Commander Voss snapped, his face contorting with rage as he slammed the tray against the door, causing Jess to flinch. "Justice always prevails. And when it does, I'll make sure your punishment is fitting."

Listening as Commander Voss stalked away, Jess trembled with fury and fear. She knew deep down that he was right: her days were numbered.

"Fuck you, Voss," she whispered to herself, her resolve hardening like steel. "I won't go down without a fight."

Chapter Eleven

Jess tossed and turned on the thin makeshift bed, her mind haunted by the man she'd killed. His dead eyes stared accusingly at her, his bloodied face twisted in a grotesque sneer.

Suddenly, the door to her cell creaked open, its rusty hinges screeching in protest. Commander Voss stood at the threshold, his expression cold and unyielding. His mere presence sent a shiver down Jess' spine, making her stomach twist into knots.

"Get up," he barked, his voice edged with disdain. "You're coming with me."

Jess scrambled to her feet, her legs shaky from days of confinement. As she followed Commander Voss through the dark underground corridor, her heart raced. Was she being taken to trial? To some other form of punishment?

"Where are we going?" she asked, her voice wavering.

"Silence!" he snapped, not sparing her a glance.

Jess swallowed hard, clenching her fists to keep them still.

They finally came to a stop outside Professor Kaplan's office. Commander Voss shoved Jess inside without ceremony. She stumbled, but managed to right herself before she fell. She looked around the room, taking in the floor-to-ceiling bookshelves and the neatly organised desk as she searched for any clues as to why she'd been brought here.

"Take a seat, Jess," Professor Kaplan commanded, his voice firm, but not unkind.

He gestured to the chair opposite his desk, and Jess obeyed, feeling like a small, frightened animal caught in a trap.

"Please wait outside, Commander Voss," the professor insisted.

Commander Voss bristled at the order, but complied, slamming the door behind him with a resounding thud.

"Jess," Professor Kaplan began, his eyes filled with concern. "I know you must be confused and scared. I want you to know that we've been working tirelessly to clear your name."

"Really?" Jess asked, her hopes tinged with disbelief. "But how? And why?"

Her fingers dug into the sides of the chair as she waited for Professor Kaplan to speak. The silence hung heavily between them, charged with anticipation. The professor leaned back in his own chair, an unreadable expression on his face as he studied Jess. Finally, he broke the silence.

"Jess, there are some things you need to know," he said, his voice carrying a gravity that made her stomach churn with anxiety. "The man you killed was a known criminal, wanted for multiple violent assaults against women. Consequently, your actions that night have been accepted as self-defence."

For a moment, Jess couldn't breathe. The words echoed in her head, a jumble of thoughts and emotions threatening to overwhelm her. Relief battled with anger, disbelief warred with hope. Her hands shook as she clutched the edge of the chair, struggling to process the revelation.

"Self-defence?" she whispered, her voice cracking. "So... I'm not in trouble?"

"No," Professor Kaplan assured.

The room seemed to sway as a deeper sense of relief crashed into Jess, disorientating her like a sudden storm. Her body shuddered with the weight of it all.

"You're free to return to your studies here at the academy," Professor Kaplan explained. "But I must warn you, there are still those who will view you as dangerous, despite the circumstances."

"Fuck them," Jess muttered under her breath.

Even as the words left her lips, she knew it wasn't that simple. The fear of being ostracised, of being seen as a monster, gnawed at her relentlessly.

"Jess," Professor Kaplan said softly, leaning forward. "You have tremendous power within you, and with that comes great responsibility. This incident can be a turning point for you – an opportunity to learn from what happened, and to grow stronger."

"Stronger?!" she scoffed, the bitter taste of anger rising in her throat as she nodded towards the office door. "How the hell am I supposed to do that when everyone's just waiting for me to fuck up again?!"

"By focusing on what you can control," Professor Kaplan stated, his voice firm but gentle. "Your training, your self-discipline, and most importantly, your relationships with those who matter. Remember, Jess, you are not alone in this fight. You have friends here, people who care about you and believe in your potential."

As the professor's words sank in, Jess felt a flicker of hope ignite within her. Maybe he was right. Maybe she could find a way to overcome the prejudice and fear that had defined so much of her life up to this point. It wouldn't be easy, and it wouldn't happen overnight. It would take time, effort, and the support of those who believed in her.

"Thank you," she said, her eyes welling up.

"There's one more person you should speak to," Professor Kaplan said, his voice steady and calm.

He picked up the phone and dialled a number, then passed the handset to Jess when someone answered.

"Jess, this is the Chief of Police," the gruff voice on the line confirmed. "I apologise for the misunderstanding."

Jess hesitated. Unsure of how to respond, she could only grasp for the right words while the anger still simmered beneath the surface. However, she knew that fury wouldn't serve her now.

"Apology noted," she managed, her voice tight with restraint.

She knew the apology was important, but it didn't erase the injustice she had faced, or the time she'd spent in that suffocating cell.

She passed the phone back to Professor Kaplan, who graciously ended the call on her behalf. She couldn't deny the lingering resentment towards those who had condemned her so quickly.

Despite the apology, the damage was done, and she couldn't forget it.

"Jess, I know it's been hard, but don't let their mistakes define you," Professor Kaplan advised, his gaze locked onto hers. "You have the power to rise above this, to take control of your own story. Don't let anyone else write it for you."

"Thank you," she replied humbly.

"Now, go and get some rest. I'll see to it that anything you might need is sent up to your room."

With a determined nod, Jess rose from her chair. The prospect of a proper sleep in a comfortable bed was too good to refuse.

Chapter Twelve

Jess stepped into one of the academy's cosy visiting rooms. The soft, golden glow of the lamps bathed the room in a warm and inviting ambience that seemed to wrap around her like a comforting embrace. Plush armchairs and sofas beckoned her to sit, but she couldn't bring herself to do so; she was too anxious, and uncertain of what to expect.

She paced back and forth, her footsteps muffled by the thick, luxurious carpet beneath her feet. Her fingers twisted and fidgeted with the hem of her shirt as she tried to calm her racing thoughts. Professor Kaplan had told her to expect a visitor this evening, but apart from that, she knew nothing else about the impending meeting.

"Fuck," she muttered under her breath.

Her eyes lingered on the door, knowing it could burst open at any second. The anticipation was killing her. Hours seemed to pass between each tick of the old-fashioned clock perched on the mantelpiece.

When the door finally opened, she couldn't believe the sight before her.

"Tom?!"

With a mixture of surprise and concern etched into his features, Jess' cousin strode towards her. Extending his arms in greeting, he couldn't help but give her a heartfelt hug.

"You have no idea how worried I've been," he said, his voice dripping with relief. "Professor Kaplan contacted me. He told me that you're here, and that you're safe."

Jess couldn't help but feel guilty at this. She was also impressed at how tirelessly Professor Kaplan must have worked to find her next of kin; she had been too afraid to give Tom's details on her enrolment form.

Fuck it! she decided. *I've already put him through too much. He deserves to know the truth.*

"Tom, I... I don't even know where to begin," she stammered, her eyes brimming with unshed tears. "I've been keeping something from you, and I'm so fucking scared that you'll hate me for it."

"Jess, whatever it is, we can handle it together," Tom reassured her, his brow furrowing in genuine concern as he took a step closer. "We're family, and nothing will change that."

"Promise?" she asked, her voice barely above a whisper.

"Promise," he confirmed, his gaze never leaving hers.

Gathering her courage, Jess took a deep breath to steady her nerves.

"Tom... I'm not like other people," she said hesitantly as she stared into his eyes, searching for any sign of rejection or disbelief. "I have powers, paranormal abilities."

As Tom's mouth fell open at the confession, Jess could see the gears turning in his head. She could only assume that he was reassessing his understanding of her experiences and struggles.

"Paranormal abilities?" he echoed, his voice wavering with uncertainty. "Are you saying you're like those people we've seen on the news? The ones who can do impossible things?"

"Yes, exactly like them," Jess confirmed. "I've been hiding it from everyone, even you. But I just couldn't keep it a secret anymore."

Her voice broke, and she bit her lip to hold back a sob.

"Things came to a head during a fucking awful shift at work," she continued. "I couldn't contain my powers any longer, and so I was arrested and brought here. Not in a bad way though. It's for the best. I was given a choice as to whether I wanted to stay and get the help I need, and, well, here I am."

Jess could see everything clicking into place within Tom's mind. No longer did he seem shocked.

"Wow, Jess, I had no idea," he said. "It must have taken a lot out of you trying to keep something like that a secret for so damn long."

"Do you hate me for it?"

"Of course not," he replied quickly, sincerity ringing in his words. "I'm just… surprised, that's all. But I'm here for you. We'll figure this out together."

With Tom's acceptance, a weight lifted from Jess' shoulders. She hadn't realised how heavy it had felt until that moment.

"Jess," Tom began, his voice gentle and soothing like a balm for a wounded soul. "I want you to know that I'm proud of you. Facing your truth like this… it takes courage."

"Thank you," she said. "Your support means everything to me. It might be a while before I can come back to the city and visit you. Paranormal Control haven't made things easy for me. It's a long story, but you have my word that I will tell you everything. No more secrets."

"I'll come and visit you at the academy," Tom said.

"Damn right you will," Jess said with a chuckle.

Relief radiating through every fibre of her being, Jess knew there would be difficult times ahead, but with Tom by her side, and with a community of fellow paranormals to support her, she was ready to face everything head-on.

As she looked out of the window and saw stars beginning to emerge in the night sky, she sighed contentedly. For the first time in a long while, she felt at ease. She now dared to believe that each new day would bring the promise of growth, self-discovery, and a brighter future – one in which she could harness her powers and shape her own destiny.